An Electrifying New Year in the Life of

Also by Val Bird and illustrated by
Rebecca Cundy

A Birthday in the Life of Ozzie Kingsford
Five (and a bit) Days in the Life of Ozzie
  Kingsford

An Electrifying New Year
in the Life of

OZZIE KINGSFORD

Val Bird

ILLUSTRATED BY
REBECCA CUNDY

RANDOM HOUSE
NEW ZEALAND

A RANDOM HOUSE BOOK published by Random House New Zealand
18 Poland Road, Glenfield, Auckland, New Zealand

For more information about our titles go to www.randomhouse.co.nz

A catalogue record for this book is available from the National Library
of New Zealand

Random House International, Random House, 20 Vauxhall Bridge Road,
London, SW1V 2SA, United Kingdom; **Random House Australia Pty Ltd,**
Level 3, 100 Pacific Highway, North Sydney 2060, Australia; **Random House
South Africa Pty Ltd,** Isle of Houghton, Corner Boundary Road and Carse
O'Gowrie, Houghton 2198, South Africa; **Random House Publishers India
Private Ltd,** 301 World Trade Tower, Hotel Intercontinental Grand Complex,
Barakhamba Lane, New Delhi 110 001, India

First published 2009

© 2009 Val Bird and Rebecca Cundy

The moral rights of the author have been asserted

ISBN 978 1 86979 156 8

Random House New Zealand uses non chlorine-bleached papers from
sustainably managed plantation forests.

Design: Anna Seabrook
Cover illustration: Rebecca Cundy
Printed in Australia by Griffin Press

The Kingsford family, and honorary
member Fletch, wish to dedicate this book
to Winsome Mitchell, creative writer,
booklover, wise lady and friend.

My Photo-Memoirs

by Oswald Devon Kingsford (who does not like his name)

(but who is the great-great-great-great-grandson of a FAMOUS EXPLORER of the same name - so for that reason I will tolerate it)

Me ↗

My Great-great-great-great-grandfather

Five (and a bit) **Days in the Life of Ozzie Kingsford**

These photos are from my last adventure which I like to call...

at first my mum was happy...

until a catastrophe occurred and my dad UNJUSTLY told us off...

My brat-sister was annoying as usual...

Luckily my BEST MATE Fletch was around to help me out during moments of complete INJUSTICE!

RUFF WUFF RUFF WUFF

and of course then there was snoops who although mostly

Partly to blame for the trouble - who could stay mad at such a cute little fella. I forgive him.

A NEW BEGINNING

The time is now exactly 8.43 am.

Tuesdays are hot

Today is Tuesday, which is the first day of the New Year.

Weather: the sun is shining.

I'm sitting in the dining room eating my HEALTHY honey wholegrain toast and at the same time attempting to do a complex mathematical calculation. It's vitally important I get this right, because according to the latest *Weirdo Weekly Wag* magazine, the number 1

end up with will be my **lucky** number for this year.

The instructions say: Find out how old the members of your family will be after their birthdays this year — write the numbers down, and then add them up.

I write down: My mother Trish says she will be thirty-four years old, but reckons she feels more like one hundred and thirty-four – Har! Har!

My dad puts his shoulders back, tucks his tummy in, and tells me he will be a youngish good-looking thirty-eight.

Our dog Snoops will be four (he turned three on Christmas day).

My friend Fletch and I will both be twelve.

Seeing Fletch is an honorary member of our family, I figure he should be counted.

My squawky-spoilt-sister Holly, (alias The Brat) will be eight horrible

years old.

I add them up, and by my reckoning they come to: **108**.

Then it says:

Divide the figure by the number of birthdays.

And that is:

108 divided by six which = eighteen.

This means that **eighteen** will be my lucky number for the whole of this year.

I hope that eighteen is a prosperous number, as my financial affairs are in a **woeful** state.

 Times have been tough.

Mum turned down my fair and reasonable request for some extra Christmas spending money.

"What is the point of me giving you my money to buy me a present?" she asked with a stern look in her eyes. "Ozzie, you HAVE to learn to think ahead. You knew Christmas was coming, so you should have put some money aside."

"But I don't get enough pocket money to save any," I protest.

"Oh, you poor poverty-stricken urchin," she said in an unsympathetic tone. "Perhaps you'd better do some extra jobs around the place to supplement your income."

Then she ruffled my hair and started singing, "*Money, money, money . . .*"

 Discussing money problems with my mother can be maddening,

infuriating and worst of all,
financially unrewarding.

Grrrrr, growl, grump, grizzle and groan,
with one added **grump** for emphasis.

A Logical Question: What is the point of
wishing people a Happy and Prosperous
New Year if you are running a zipped-purse
policy?

Last night we sat up and watched the New
Year arrive.

This was after going out to our cousins'
(The Three Geekiest Geeks) for tea.

We were **supposed** to stay and wait for
the New Year at their place, but my sister

The Brat had a squabble session with Cousin Miriam.

Horror story: It was reported that my sister used fisticuffs to settle a point of difference.

Miriam came running into the room crying a humungous heap of real tears and squawking, "WAHHHH WAHHHH! Holly hit me!"

Next second, The Brat arrived.

She was wearing a mean face with squinted-up eyes.

"Miriam hit me first," she shouted. "I only hit her back as hard as she hit me."

Miriam started crying even louder.

"I did not hit her," she screamed. "Holly's telling fibs."

The Brat then turned red in the face and shrieked: "I am not fibbing! I don't like you any more, you're a mean, horrible, fibbing dummy-bummy."

Under these circumstances I reckon it was perfectly natural for our mum to suffer from **acute exasperation** mixed with a near fatal dose of parental humiliation.

After apologising forty-eight thousand times, Mum said to Dad, "Come on, I think we should take Holly home to bed."

 I was sort of pleased to be leaving early, as keeping company with brain-box geeks brings on a feeling of **educational inequality**.

When we arrived home **The Brat** was sent straight to bed, but I was given **the thumbs**

up
and Mum
said, "Come on
Ozzie . . . let's sit
out in the courtyard
and wait for the New Year to arrive."

And while it was very pleasant sitting
outside looking at the moon and the twinkling
stars, I'm sorry to report there were no
significant changes to the world when my
multi-functional solar powered watch
displayed the magical midnight hour.

No stars fell down from the heavens.
The world did not stop revolving.

No mysterious spooky ghosts appeared in the dark of the night.

There was No almighty clap-bang of thunder.

Or wicked bolts of fork lightning.

I thought those mischievous forest sprites might come sneaking around . . .

But they didn't.

All that happened was Dad kissed Mum.

She passed the kiss on to me . . .

I went to pass the kiss on to doggy Snoops, but found he was snoring under the table. I prodded him with my foot; he made a *wiff, wuffy, huffy,* stop-prodding-me noise, and didn't even bother to wake up. Apart from a distant sound of someone letting off firecrackers . . . that was it.

Dad was up and about early today.

That's because he's gone off for three days with a bunch of his golfing buddies to play in the *Bay Middle-Aged-to-Veteran New Year Golf Tournament.*

Last night he told us:

"I'll sneak off quietly in the morning so you lot can have a sleep-in."

But when Mister Wally came to pick him up, he roared his big V8 up the driveway and hooted his car horn so it woke us all up.

Next thing we hear Dad yelling out in a

booming **foghorn** voice:

"HAS ANYBODY SEEN MY WALLET . . . ?"

In the end, we **all** had to get out of bed and help him look.

 For a grown-up person he can make an **awful** racket.

Even Snoops scampered about the place with his nose to the ground . . .

Mum finally found his wallet in the bathroom hiding behind a box of tissues; she rolled her eyes and grumped, "So much for the sleep-in."

Mum says she doesn't mind Dad going away — and that we will have a few **quiet days**

to ourselves — but I think she's just putting on an act, as when he left I saw her glaring at his collection of golf trophies and muttering to herself.

The time is now 8.55 am, and I'm eating my

last piece of **healthy** honey wholegrain toast when Mum comes into the room.

She sighs and says, "Oh my giddiness, I'm suffering from **exhaustion**," and flops herself down in the nearest chair. "It's just as well your father has promised us a week away after the tournament — only *five* more days to go."

She picks up the pamphlets of the *Luxury Holiday Resort* and gazes at them for a lengthy time.

I sigh, "Yeah, I'm really looking forward to it. I like the

sound of the luxury bit."

Mum smiles. "I thought you would," she says. "In the meantime I hope you can find something to do with yourself, and don't expect me to amuse you."

"Fletch and I've got plans," I tell her. "His nana is still laid up, so he's stuck at home. We're going to do stuff together."

"What sort of stuff?" Mum enquires.

"Top secret, scientific experimental stuff."

"Mmm," she says, "I'm not sure I like the sound of that."

"Dad said we could use his workshop," I tell her while trying to keep a truthful expression on my face.

"Did he?" Mum questions, and fortunately (which saves me from having to tell a double-fibber) right at that moment our dog Snoops runs into the room. His little eyes are all bright and happy because I told him I would take him for a walk when I had finished my breakfast, and right behind him comes my sister.

The Brat has just finished washing her hair and it is still drip-drip-dripping all over the place . . . she's put on her yellow shorts with a black top, and for some weirdo reason has stuck her Buzzy Bee Club antenna on top of her wet head.

It must be said: she looks like a seriously wet drippy twit.

Mum gives her an exasperated look and says, "Holly, will you please dry your hair — look, you're wetting everything!"

Holly gives Mum a grumpy look and says, "I don't want to dry it — I like it wet."

Mum's eyes harden and I can see there's female trouble brewing, so I say to Snoops in a man-to-man voice, "Come on, boy, let's get out of here."

ROCKY TIMES ONE

The time is now exactly 9.05 am.

Weather: the sun is shining, and the temperature is 19 degrees Celsius.

 It's going to be a hot one.

Snoops and I walk around the block, then through the park to Fletch's house.

We find him out in the garage. He's rounded up the **necessary components** for our scientific experiment and plonked them in a big cardboard box, which he's loaded onto his old buggy.

"I've got Mum's old vacuum cleaner, it's heavy-as, so we need wheels to transport this lot," he explains. "And then we can use the buggy for transporting the ESM." (For your information, ESM stands for Electricity Storage Machine.)

The project we're about to undertake is one Fletch read about in one of my *Weirdo Weekly Wag* magazines — which pointed out that around the world, two thousand thunderstorms produce more than eight million lightning bolts on an average day.

(For further information on this subject, Google "weather".)

We are (that is Fletch and I) going to build a machine to store the electricity from the storms. The electricity will be held in the vacuum cleaner's dust compartment until needed. When I ask Fletch how we get the electricity back out again, he said we will worry about that problem when we get to it.

Plans for construction of a miniature ESM.

As invented by Fletch Jessup.
In consultation with Ozzie Kingsford.

1 Take possession of one functioning vacuum cleaner.

2 The dust-bag part of the cleaner must be redesigned to store the electricity (that will be suctioned from the lightning bolts).

3 The plug-in cord must be waterproofed — or else we could get an electric shock.

4 The cleaner, which will from now on be

referred to as an ESM, must be installed in a waterproof container — with a hole bored for suction (which must be facing upwards).

5 Fletch's old buggy will be used to provide a construction base, and then used to transport the ESM to suitable sites.

6 When an electrical storm strikes, the ESM operator turns on the machine and the energy will be sucked up and stored until needed.

"What's to stop the electricity from coming straight back out the hose pipe?" I enquire.

"Well," says Fletch in a technical tone of voice, "I reckon that it will sink to the bottom and stay there."

"How come?" I ask.

"Because it must be heavy — otherwise,

if electricity was lightweight, it would float around giving us electric shocks. I'm sure I heard my dad going on about it one day."

I ponder that theory, but seeing as I can't come up with anything to dispute the reasoning behind it, and as Fletch's dad is a policy advisor to the government, I feel I must accept it — but then again, this could be due to my **electrical inexperience**.

There's one worrying thought about this whole experimental business — and that is Fletch's idea that the ESM will find a home on the decking outside my bedroom.

"That way, we can run the power cord through your window."

"Why not set it up at your place?" I question.

"Because my bedroom is upstairs," he replies. "And we'd need an awful long cord to plug it in with — and as a bonus, it never rains on your decking, which means cutting back the chances of accidental electrocution."

"Jeepers — I dunno if Mum's going to like

all this stuff out on her decking," I complain. "That's where she keeps her potted plant collection."

"We'll have to convince her that this is an educational project," Fletch declares in a firm, unwavering voice. "After all, she's a school teacher so she should be encouraging us to expand our knowledge — and we can always cut her in on some of the profits when we sell the energy back to the national grid."

"How much do they pay?" I ask.

"I'm not sure," he replies. "But Mum reckons our power bill keeps sky-rocketing, and so we should be looking at the big-time money bracket. I reckon once we get a super-size model operating we could be looking at a hundred thousand dollars a year."

"Fair go?" I question.

"Well," Fletch says (while doing some

mental mathematical calculations), "maybe fifty thousand each might be more like it."

"That sounds okay to me," I say. "But there's one thing I want to know: how do we get the electricity into the national grid?"

"I dunno," he confesses. "I haven't read up on that bit yet, but we'll work it out."

I have to say there seem to be an awful lot of UNKNOWNS attached to this particular project, but as Fletch is my mate, and fifty thousand dollars is a heck of a lot of money, I will provide him with all the support he needs.

We're nearly home, and are just walking by the house next door (where Missus Hobbs lives) when we hear her call out, "Yoooooooooooo hooooooooooo, boys."

She comes walking towards us and I can see by the glint in her eyes she's lining us up for volunteer duty of some sort — Missus Hobbs bends down to pat Snoops.

"And how are you, my little ratbag?" she questions.

Snoops whimpers, "*Wiff, wuff, wuff,*" and licks her hand.

"What on earth have you got there?" Missus Hobbs asks while pointing to the box of stuff on the buggy.

"It's specialised equipment for a scientific experiment," I tell her.

"That sounds interesting," she says. "It's good that you're doing something educational." Then she puts a hand out and ruffles my hair. "But, my young friend, I've just been talking to your mother. I'm pulling apart my rock garden and turning it into lawn and she tells me that she'd like the rocks for her garden."

Then she gives us a big, beaming smile . . .

"So come over, and bring your wheelbarrow." And then she turns to Fletch and says, "And this young man can use mine."

Mum says she wants the rocks stacked around the back.

Right down the end of the section!

It's at this very moment I have an **inspirational** thought.

"Mum, I reckon a rock garden would look better around the front."

"Mmm," she says while giving me a razor-sharp look, "and that way you wouldn't have to cart the rocks so far. Would you?"

"That's got nothing to do with it," I protest while putting on an offended expression. "I reckon we should wait until Dad comes home and ask him."

She shakes her head and says, "No, we're not having a rock garden around the front, so I suggest you rock-movers get cracking right now, and remember, *the sooner you start, the sooner you finish.*"

"Jeepers," says Fletch as we head back to load up rocks for the third time, "it would have to be the furtherest point — how come every time I come to your place we end up with a million jobs to do?"

I sigh. "Consider yourself lucky you're only an honorary member of the family," I tell him. "I have to live here full-time!

I reckon it's like living in a slave-labour camp — I sent a Christmas card to the local Chairperson of the United Nations Child Protection Foundation with a letter outlining my problems, but I haven't heard anything back yet."

Fletch points to the pile of rocks that we still have to move. "I reckon by the time we've finished moving this lot we could be suffering from a condition known as juvenile overwork syndrome, which I am told could possibly retard our growth, deform our bones and leave us emotionally and physically scarred for life."

"Jeez," I say to Fletch, "absolute radical stuff — who told you that?"

"I dunno," he replies while shrugging his shoulders. "But I'm sure somebody must have said it — or else how would I know about it?"

 There are times when talking to Fletch can lead to a state of mental confusion.

It's at this confused moment I see an old tea chest stacked in Missus Hobbs' wood shed.

"Hey," I say to Fletch, "do you think that

could make
the outer
casing for our
electrifying
machine?"

Fletch's eyes light up.

"I reckon it would be perfect," he says. "We can paint flower pictures on the outside of it, put it into place on the decking, and tell your mum we made it especially for her."

"Good thinking. Mum likes flowery stuff," I say. "But YOU can ask Missus Hobbs if we can have it."

"Why don't YOU ask her?" Fletch questions.

"Because," I tell him, "I'm just the kid next door. You are an impressive visitor."

"Am I impressive?" Fletch asks.

"Well," I say, "you WILL be if you can

persuade Missus Hobbs to part with that tea chest. She's not normally a give-it-away type person."

 I must make a point of studying Fletch's persuasive techniques.

I'm totally amazed, flabbergasted and dumbfounded.

Not only did Missus Hobbs say we can have the tea chest, she gives Fletch a beaming smile and takes us into her shed where she finds some paint for us to decorate it with.

"What a nice lad you are," she tells Fletch (while ignoring me) and then raves on about how much my mother will appreciate this thoughtful, creative gift. "Now remember," she says almost as an afterthought, "these are high-gloss paints, so don't go splashing them all over the place — you must be careful."

Fletch and I give her the thumbs up.

"We promise," we say in unison as we make off with our prized possessions.

We're about to smuggle the tea chest into the workshop, when unfortunately Mum spots us. We quickly shove it in the door at the same moment as she pokes her head out the back door.

"What have you boys got there?" she enquires in an extra suspicious tone of voice.

"Nothing much," I profess. "It's just a necessary component for our scientific experiment."

"Are you sure Dad said you can use his workshop?" she questions in an even more extra suspicious tone.

I cross my fingers behind my back, and silently fast-count to eighteen (which is my lucky number) before replying with a hopefully believable, "Yes, Mum." Fletch puts on his innocent face (which Mum falls for every time).

"Okay," she says. "I'll take your word for it — but you better not be telling me porkies."

"Who, me?" I say. "I'll have you know honesty is my middle name."

Mum rolls her eyes, but is obviously lost for words as her head disappears back into the great indoors.

MUM GETS SOME NEWS

Today is Wednesday the second day of the New Year.

The time is 7.36 am and I've just woken up.

Weather: I pull my curtains and the sun shines in.

Snoops yawns, and then gives me a tail wag. Yesterday we undercoated the tea chest.

Today Fletch is coming around at 9.30 am and we'll start painting the decorations on it. Before Fletch went home we practised drawing flowers, and came up with a pink, blue, green and yellow design that Mum will find totally irresistible, and that will make her friends envious.

Then I remember: Last night I saw Dad in my dreams.

He was dripping wet and his head was covered in lake weed.

 I wonder what this means?

And as I think that particular thought, there comes a loud banshee scream . . .

"Ahhhhhhh! Look what's happened to my Barbie! WAAAAAAHH!"

My bedroom door flies open . . . and there stands a horrible sight known as:

THE BRAT.

She's wearing her spotty nightdress and is waving a mutilated Barbie mermaid doll in the air. "Snoops chewed the tail off my doll. He's a naughty-bad-mean dog!"

Snoops, sensing trouble, and being a coward at heart, makes a dive under the duvet cover. The Brat continues to advance with a vengeful look in her eye.

Then Mum arrives on the scene . . .

"What's going on here?" she asks. "What's this dreadful noise all about?"

The Brat waves the doll around and proceeds to carry on with her wobbly . . .

"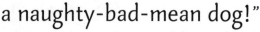 Snoops killed my doll, he's chewed her tail and now she's

dead, and she's my best-ever doll.
WAAAAAAAHH!"

"Stop that squawking," Mum commands.

Sensing I have a role to play, I put on my official Ultimate Defence Attorney Voice.

"How do you know Snoops did it?" I question. "It could've been Cougar Cat from next door, or some other wandering animal — you're jumping to conclusions, and I reckon you owe our loyal and faithful dog an apology."

My voice must have a ring of authority because The Brat stops squawking and gives me a puzzled look.

"But he's ALWAYS chewing up my toys," she protests.

"Have you ever seen him do it?" I question.

"No," she confesses, "but it's his teeth marks."

"**Prove it**," I tell her. "And look what your squawking has done to this **innocent** creature." I pull back the duvet cover and expose a . . .

Sad eyed.

Tremulous.

Pedigree Highland Terrier.

Whose little tail is **not wagging**.

"This good natured animal is displaying signs of **extreme** stress," I exclaim while pointing a serious finger at The Brat. "You've hurt his feelings, and now he's heartbroken."

Mum gives me an amused smile, folds her arms and says in a thoughtful tone of voice, "Ozzie, what an **impressive** performance — remind me to enrol you for Law School." She's about to say more when the phone in the hallway rings and she immediately dashes off to answer it. The Brat, who's now a reformed villain, is patting Snoops and apologising for scaring him.

"Sorry, Snoops, I didn't mean to hurt your feelings," she says in her squeaky voice.

While Snoops is saying (in our secret doggy language):

"Har wuffy har, har! — I like *eating Barbie dolls. If you leave them lying around the place, I'll* chomp *them to pieces with my sharp teeth — har, wuffy, har, har!"*

When Mum walks back into the room, she looks extremely exasperated.

"What's the matter?" I ask.

"Oh my double giddiness," she says as she flops down on my bed.

"It's your dad. He got whacked on the

head by a golf ball.
He's spent the night
in hospital, but apart
from a temporary memory
loss he should be all right
. . . Mister Wally is
bringing him home."

The Brat stops patting
Snoops, she leans forward and says,

"Oh! Poor Daddy."

Mum sighs. "What about poor Mummy?"
she asks in a disheartened tone of voice.
"They say he's being good natured at the
moment, but can you imagine how grumpy
he's going to be when his memory returns and
he discovers that all he brought home was a
bump on the head, and no trophy!"

(For further information on this subject,
Google "bear with a sore head".)

■48

"Don't forget," says The Brat suddenly becoming animated, "I've got Primrose coming around to play for the whole day today, and she's going to bring all her Barbies and we're going to have a DOLL PARTY."

I watch Mum turn pale with apprehension — having Pernickety Primrose Perkins and a bumped-on-the-head-golf-nutter in the house at the same time does not seem like a good idea.

 By the look on my mother's face you could say it's a very unfortunate idea indeed.

TRIPLE TROUBLE

everything happens at 9.47 am.

I've just finished playing chuck-the-ball for Snoops.

Weather: a big cloud comes over the sun.

Fletch walks up our driveway. He is carrying a shoe box and he gives me the thumbs up.

"I raided my dad's shed," he tells me. "I've got some waterproofing stuff and enough insulation tape to see the job done properly."

"That's good," I say. "Righto, it's off to work we go!"

But at that very moment Missus Perkins' red car turns up our driveway.

Fletch, who has the ability to recognise trouble when he sees it, says, "Critical stuff, look who's arrived — I'll leave you to it, har! har!" and abandons me.

 This is hardly the behaviour of a true and loyal friend.

Missus Perkins opens the car door, and climbs out . . . she's wearing a frilly red dress and the highest high heels I've ever seen.

"Hello, Ozzie," she says in a high-pitched

voice. "And how are you today?"

"I'm okay," I tell her.

She clickety-click-high-heel-walks around the passenger side of the car and helps **the delicate Pernickety Primrose** to get out. Primrose is dressed in a horrible pink Barbie doll outfit, with ribbons in her hair, and I reckon she's wearing the type of shoes that ballerinas wear.

Missus Perkins unloads a heap of pink Barbie storage boxes from the back seat. "Would you be a *sweetie-darling* boy," she oozes, "and carry these inside for me."

At that moment Mum walks out the back door with **The Brat** in hot pursuit.

Mum's about to say something, but Missus Perkins speaks first.

"Hello, Trish," she says in an **efficient** tone of voice. "Sorry, I can't stop to chat. I've got a charity garden tour on this morning."

She hands Mum a piece of paper.

"These are Primrose's dietary requirements for the day, and a list of what Barbie dolls she's brought with her. Could you please check she doesn't leave any dolls behind — also don't let her play in the direct sunshine, and a wee rest mid-afternoon is a good idea . . . I'll pick her up at around sixish, I presume you don't mind giving her an evening meal, but NO fried food — and make sure she drinks at least three glasses of water — NO fizzy or cordial."

She blows Primrose an air kiss so she doesn't smudge her lipstick, hops back in her car and reverses out the driveway leaving Mum standing there looking totally flabbergasted.

The flabbergasted expression has not had

time to wear off Mum's face when Mister
Wally's big black V8 roars up our driveway.

Mister Wally gets out of the car.

He gives Mum a sort of apologetic smile . . .

"Sorry about this," he says.

Mum's eyes go straight to where Dad
sits in the backseat — from where I'm
standing I can see he's got a white bandage
around his head, and he's smiling a dopey-
looking smile.

Mum looks in the car window . . . then
turns to Mister Wally. "I know you said he
got whacked on the head, but why's his arm
in a sling?"

"Well," says Mister Wally, "when the
golf ball hit him he was standing on the
edge of the lake water-feature hole, and
unfortunately he fell in."

(It's then I remember my dream!)

"That still doesn't explain the sling," Mum says, narrowing her eyes.

"Ummm, yep, well," says Mister Wally, who's starting to turn red in the face. "What happened was when we were hauling him out of the lake, we must've wrenched his shoulder. The doctor thinks it should come right with a bit of rest . . . but his foot's going to give him some mobility problems until the pain and bruising wear off."

"And please, do tell me what happened to his foot?"

 Mum's voice is rising to absolute exasperation level.

"Ummm, ummm," says Mister Wally. "It's like this, Archie was backing up the golf cart so we could load him onto it . . . but in the process he ran over your husband's foot, just one of those **unfortunate** happenings — but you'll be pleased to know all the accident compensation forms have been processed."

Mum gives Mister Wally one of her **very false smiles**, but I can hear the growl of a **wild tigress** rattling about in the back of her throat.

"Thank you for returning him to us," she says in a strained voice.

Mister Wally looks at his watch. "I'll give you a hand to get him inside, but I'd better not dally," he says. "I'm paired off for an afternoon round."

The Brat takes Primrose off to her bedroom to be introduced to her army of Barbie dolls, while I help Mum settle Dad on the couch in the lounge. She puts his feet up; I put a soft pillow under his head.

Mum covers him with a soft blanket.

"How are you feeling?" she asks with a concerned look on her face.

"Yes, dear," Dad replies with a goofy grin.

"Yes what?" Mum asks while giving him a puzzled look.

"Yes, dear," says Dad, and this time he winks at her.

Mum looks at me; I look at her, and I'm sure we're both thinking the same thought:

Is Dad slightly cuckoo — or is he pulling our legs?

Mum folds her arms, purses her lips, looks at him fixedly and tries again.

CUCKOO!

"Darling, are you hungry?"

"Yes, dear," he says.

"Are you tired?"

"Yes, dear," says Dad and gives a big open-mouth yawn.

"Mmm," says Mum. "Tell me this, can you say anything else other than 'yes, dear'?"

"Yes, dear," says Dad.

"Mmm," says Mum while turning her attention to me. "I see what they mean about him being good natured. Your father is obviously stuck on the 'yes' word. I wonder how long it will last for?"

"WOW! Radical stuff," I say. "I better get in quick before it wears off, I reckon this would be the **perfect** time to hit him up for an increase in pocket money."

DETECTING TROUBLE

7 he time is 10.46 am.

After my mother accuses me of being a heartless money-hungry mercenary and attempting to take advantage of my father's confused state of mind, I depart the scene and go to the workshop to help Fletch.

In my absence, Fletch has given the tea chest another undercoat, and tells me that later this afternoon we can start the artistic design work.

UNFORTUNATELY Snoops helped with the undercoating and he's got white paint on the left-hand-side of his body.

"Don't worry about it," I tell Fletch, "he got undercoated once before when Dad was painting the laundry. It wore off after a bit."

"How are you going to explain it to your mum?" Fletch asks.

"She won't even notice," I tell him. "She's too busy worrying about Dad."

"Righto," says Fletch. "I'll take your word for it."

"So what comes next?" I ask.

"Well," he says, "I'm going to waterproof the vacuum cleaner bags. I've got a professional, money-back-fully-guaranteed water-proofing substance, and I reckon three coats should do it. I'll do some spare bags for when we change them over

— and you can wrap the electrical cords with insulation tape. Just to be on the safe side, we'll spray a waterproof coating over them as well."

It's exactly 11.37 am when those jobs are finished and I get out Dad's electric drill.

 This is the first time I've used an electric drill.

 There has to be a first time for everything.

 I passed the *Weirdo Weekly Wag* **Home Handyman Competence Test** with an eighty per cent quality rating.

I turn up the radio extra loud to drown out the drill noise, and Fletch stands against the door (in case of unwanted visitors).

After attempting to copy my father's drilling techniques I manage to bore a hole in the side of the box — but the hole is much too small.

I don't know how to change the drill bit, so I bore a series of holes around the first hole, until the box sort of disintegrates enough to thread the plug-bit through.

I then repeat this procedure on the lid of the tea chest, so there's a hole for the electricity to make an entry.

Next up, we put the vacuum cleaner in the tea chest; Fletch holds it in place while I jam bits of wood from our firewood heap around it so it will stay in the required position.

We give the box a jiggle, and nothing collapses.

"Phew," I say. "It looks likes it's going to stay in place — we have done it!"

"Yay!" yells Fletch. "We are overloaded with intellect!"

We give each other an approving grin.

Next up, we open the tins of paint that Missus Hobbs gave us.

These tins must have been sitting around for a million-or-so years as all the paint is thick like porridge.

"I know how to fix this," I tell Fletch.

I very slowly add eighteen squirts of water (my lucky number), while Fletch stirs the paint until it is fluid enough for the required brushwork. We test it out on an old bit of wood . . .

"Right on," says Fletch. "Action stations ahead."

"Yeah," I say. "But first let's go and get

some food, or I might drop dead from lack of nutrition."

"Should we put the lids back on the paint?" Fletch asks.

"Nah," I say. "She'll be right."

For lunch we eat cheese toasted sandwiches with mustard pickles, tomato and leftover kumara mash. Mum's sitting at the table looking at the holiday brochures.

 She looks a bit **depressed.**

I ask, "Are you all right, Mum?"

"I think we should cancel our holiday," she says in a sad voice.

"Why?"

"Because your dad's a wreck — it must have been an elephant-sized golf cart that ran over his foot, and he moans if I so much as touch his shoulder." She sighs. "And if he says 'Yes, dear' one more time I shall go stark raving nutty myself."

She shows me the small print on the brochure . . .

"If we cancel now, we get our deposit back, but if we leave it another day — then all that money goes down the drain." She gives another big sigh. "But we did promise you kids a holiday."

I swallow a lump of disappointment and say, "It's okay, Fletch and me have got things to do. Don't worry about us."

"Are you sure?" she asks while picking up the telephone.

"Yep," I say. "We've got a huge educational project underway and I don't know if I could handle all that luxury stuff. I'm a rough and rugged type at heart."

She smiles and reaches out a hand and ruffles my hair. "Thank you for making my decision stress-free," she says.

After Mum has talked to the holiday booking agent, Fletch gives Mum an enquiring look.

"Talking of stress," he says, "where are the two Barbie nutters? It's awfully quiet in here."

"They've been banished to the outdoor playhouse," Mum says. "But do me a favour and keep an eye out for trouble."

At that very moment the wind comes up

and the back door slams shut . . . BANG!

And in the distance I hear it — the sound of the forest sprites' laughter.

"Har! Har! Har!"

 These mischievous sprites have been following me around since my eleventh birthday, and their laughter is usually a warning of trouble to come!

"Do you mean to say, those girls are out the back, and we are in here?" I question.

"That's exactly what I said," Mum says. "Why?"

Fletch and I both look at each other with eyes wide open . . .

The hairs on my legs stand up.

My trouble detector starts rapidly

beep-beeping.

I'm off the kitchen chair and out the back door at a speed of *two million miles an hour*. I run so fast that my legs set a new land speed record . . .

I stop by the playhouse only to find it **empty**, that is apart from Snoops who's sitting in the middle of the floor surrounded by a pile of chewed-up Barbie dolls. At present he's chomping the legs of a bridal doll.

He gives me a wide-eyed startled look.

"You're a *mean Barbie-destroying machine!*" I tell him. "But keep up the good work and I will prepare the case for your defence."

This time I dash straight for Dad's workshop. I fling open the door. And there's a sight I did not want to see.

The Brat is holding a paintbrush, which is **dripping** pink paint . . . and when I see what she's been painting, the blood runs cold in my once warm veins.

The Brat's case for her defence,
as prepared by herself:

 I asked Dad if I could play in his workshop, and he said "Yes, dear".

 I thought the paints were like the ones we use at school.

How am I to know that they would not wash off easy-as?

 It was Primrose's idea to paint spots on our faces.

 And **Primrose said** she wanted her hair painted pink, because she wanted to be **a pink Barbie princess.**

 And if Ozzie didn't want anybody to use his paints, HE should have put **them away.**

 And it was MUM who told us to play outside, so it's all really her fault.

Snoops' case for his defence,
as put forward by Ozzie Devon Kingsford, who is the great-great-great-great-grandson of a world-famous explorer:

 This highly intelligent Pedigree Highland Terrier only chewed up thirteen Barbie dolls (out of a total of thirty-eight), six of which he then buried in the garden for safekeeping.

 He **could** have chewed up more if he had wanted to.

 Therefore, he should be **congratulated** for showing restraint.

 And finally, if the girls didn't want their Barbie dolls chewed up, they should have put them away.

SETTING THE SCENE

Today is Thursday, which is the third day of the New Year. The time is 8.32 am.

Weather: it's clouded over and the weatherman is forecasting some rain later in the day.

Mum and I are sitting in the dining room eating **healthy** breakfast cereal.

Dad and **The Brat** are sharing the couch, while they munch honey toast and watch cartoons on television.

"Do you know what?" Mum asks in a thoughtful tone of voice.

"No," I say. "I don't know anybody called *what*."

"Don't be a smarty-party," Mum says while rolling her eyes at me. "What I was going to say is, I think Snoops has changed colour, either that or he's prematurely ageing."

I look to where Snoops is sitting with his undercoated side in clear view.

"Maybe the girls painted him too," I suggest with an innocent air.

"Mmm," says Mum, "I always wanted a half-black and half-white dog. Anyway it has to be an improvement on a pink Primrose."

"You're right," I say in an agreeable voice. "And I reckon once the story gets out that Holly has taken up body and hair painting, she'll be declared an **artistic hazard** and nobody will be allowed to come and play with her."

A little glint of humour sparks out of Mum's left eye.

"I wonder how much of Primrose's hair had to be chopped off," she ponders.

"Quite a bit, I would think — she might've ended up with a *number one*."

"Mmm," Mum says, with just a wee hint of a wicked smile, "I suppose it's possible. Your sister managed to give her a good, solid coating."

"Missus Perkins just about blew up like dynamite when she saw the chomped-up Barbie dolls," I tell Mum. "But she got even madder when she saw killer-dog Snoops, who had heaps of blonde hairs sticking out of his choppers — her face went red as, and her eyes were like lightning bolts of fury."

As I say those very words, I see a blonde head go past our dining room window that I recognise as belonging to Fletch, and then I hear a knock on the door.

"COME IN IF YOU ARE RICH OR GOOD LOOKING," I yell out.

"Ozzie," Mum reprimands, "get up and answer the door **properly**!"

But it's too late to be **proper**, because Fletch heard my voice and now his head pops around the dining room door.

"Gidday," I say.

"Hello, Fletch," says Mum while waving her hand over the remainder of the food that's sitting on the table. "Help yourself if you want something to eat."

"Thanks all the same, but I've had breakfast," Fletch says and gives my mother a smile. Then he turns to me. "I heard the weather forecast and they are talking about thunderstorms tonight, so I figure we should get an early start."

Mum looks puzzled, "What's thunder got to do with getting an early start?"

Fletch gives Mum a very serious look.

"I'm sorry, Madam, we can't give out any information until we've tested our invention." Then he gives her one of his charming smiles and asks, "Is it okay if I invite myself to sleep over tonight?"

"Of course you can stay," Mum says with a curious look on her face, "but I'd love to know what you two are up to."

"Mum," I say, "if you want to know what we're doing, then you need to become an **Official Shareholder** in our new company, which, I assure you, will eventually end up making millions of dollars."

"Is that right?" asks Mum, tapping the table with her fingers. "And what do I have to do to become a partner?"

I look at Fletch, "Whaddya reckon? If she gave us fifty bucks each, would that be enough for starters?"

■■◣

"That was a good try," Fletch says as we walk out to the workshop. "Some ready money would've been handy."

"Yeah," I tell him. "But she didn't have to laugh quite so much. After all she's the one who encourages us to use inventive thinking."

Fletch nods. "Sometimes parents underestimate their children's potential, and it's said this situation can be remedied by drawing similarities to one's own childhood experiences, but due to a mental blockage caused by ageing it's difficult to break through this barrier."

"Wicked stuff," I say. "Who told you that?"

For a moment Fletch looks baffled, and then he confesses, "I dunno. I guess it must be an ingrained thought I picked up from somewhere."

"Helpers," I encourage. "If we put all your ingrained thoughts together, then we could be major contributors to the newly formed *Weirdo Weekly Wag*'s Misunderstood Weirdos Group."

"You reckon?"

"Yep, and they pay good money."

"Do they?"

"The *contributor of the week* gets ten dollars. I could be your agent and we can split the proceeds fifty-fifty."

"Well," says Fletch, giving me a proud smile, "when we get this ESM working, then perhaps we should start concentrating on the philosophical side of my personality."

We have a problem: The Brat used up nearly all the pink paint, so we have to rethink our flower design for the tea chest.

"We can work on opposite sides, and create as we go," Fletch suggests. "We can't be too ambitious if we're going to catch tonight's thunderstorm. Is your mother into modern art?"

"You mean like splodge, splatter, dab, and blob?"

Fletch grins and gives me the thumbs up,

"You got it," he says.

"Well," I say, "I once heard her say she likes Picasso."

"Radical," says Fletch. "I reckon if we **splatter** and **blob**, then stick an odd hand, foot and eyeball in amongst the **splodges**, she will be beside herself with modernistic joy."

It's lunchtime when we finish painting our masterpieces.

We stand back and admire our handiwork.

"It looks good to me," I comment.

"You've got a radical combination of splatters."

"Yeah," says Fletch.

"I like your blue eye, with the daisy centre. That's known as free-spirited inventive stuff."

"Mum likes blue and yellow," I tell Fletch while secretly puffing up with artistic pride. "We need to leave the paint to dry," I say. "So after lunch shall we go to your place and get your pyjamas? We can take Snoops for a walk."

"Good thinking," Fletch replies.

It's 3.25 pm when we get back from Fletch's house.

Already the sky is starting to blacken up over in the west.

But we find the paint on the tea chest is still not dry.

"We'll just have to be careful how we load

it on the buggy," Fletch says. "Make sure you keep your fingers off the wettest bits of paint."

But when we try to pick it up, we find it's too heavy to lift.

So we have to:

Take the firewood out of the tea chest.

Take out the vacuum cleaner.

Sneak-sneakily transport the tea chest onto the decking.

Stuff the vacuum cleaner back in.

Jam the firewood around it.

Put the lid on.

Arrange Mum's pot plants on top of and around it (so it looks like it's there for a reason).

Then:

We put the cord through my bedroom window.

I plug it in and turn it on.

Fletch yells out, "**YaHOOOO**, it goes."

Which means: We're ready for action.

We wait until after tea before showing Mum
her present.

Dad's having a sleep on the couch; Snoops
is curled up next to him.

The Brat's putting her Barbie dolls to bed.

Fletch and I help clean up in the kitchen.

I reckon the timing is perfect . . .

I wink at Fletch and give him a questioning
look.

He gives me the nod.

I take hold of Mum's hand and say, "Hey,
Mum, come and see what our secret project
is all about."

"Yeah," says Fletch. "It's a present especially for you."

"For me?" Mum questions with a surprised look on her face. "One minute you're hitting me up for money, the next minute you're giving me gifts. May I ask what exactly you're attempting to soften me up for?"

"Mum," I say in an offended tone of voice, "you do NOT have a trusting personality. Look at my honest face — I am your first-born child, why would you think that I'm softening you up?"

"Mmm, please excuse my suspicious nature. Righto boys," she says as she holds out her hands, "and just to show how much I do trust you, I'll close my eyes and you can lead me forth."

I take hold of one of her hands, and Fletch takes the other.

We go out the back door.

"Be careful down the steps," I tell her.

We walk up the driveway, and when we're standing next to the decking I say, "Okay, Mum, you can open your eyes now."

We watch as her sight focuses on the **magnificent tea chest**.

Her eyes *flicker*, then they *flicker* again . . .

A puzzled look *zooms* across her face.

"My giddiness," she says, her voice comes out sounding slightly croaky.

She walks slowly up the steps onto the decking . . .

She looks at the box from one angle, then from another, she frowns, she closes one eye, she looks again, and then she starts to smile.

"How long did you boys spend on this?"

"Years," says Fletch. "It's taken a lot of creative talent."

"Yeah," I say, "we're thinking of going into an arty business."

"Well," Mum enthuses, "it must be said it's one of a kind. I can honestly say I've never seen anything quite like it before, and probably **never** will again."

It's fortunate that Mum's happy to look at her present from a distance, which means she does not catch sight of the cord that's poking out the other side.

"*Phew*," says Fletch when she finally leaves to go back inside the house, "if that was my mother she would've had us lifting it about so she could examine every square inch of the thing."

"Yeah," I say, "but your mother's a perfectionist, mine sort of ambles along through the corridors of life bossing people around."

"And talking of perfection," Fletch says, "there's one thing missing. We need a lightning attractor. Do you reckon we can snitch one of your dad's fishing rods?"

"I don't see why not," I reply. "We can stick it up when it gets dark, and put it back in the morning and no one will ever know."

It's when I say those very words a wicked

wind blows from the west.

I feel the earth shake as dark clouds start to swirl about.

A shiver runs up my spine — then I hear it.

The sound of those pesky forest sprites:

"Har! Har! Har!"

And helpers, they don't sound very far away!

Fletch and I look at each other.

"Critical stuff," he says. "I wonder what that lot are planning."

"I dare say we will soon find out. I just hope it's nothing too revolutionary," I say in a negative voice.

We have a family tea sitting up at the table.

Mum has cooked a chook and we have

salad, cheese bread, mustard pickles, hard-boiled eggs and tomatoes.

 Dad is still goofy.

 He just smiles and agrees with what everybody says.

 I reckon Dad's goofiness is starting to try Mum's patience.

I think if he doesn't return to his mean, crotchety, tyrannical old self soon, then Mum may develop a dose of life-threatening exasperation.

 There have been SOME changes:

Dad's taken off his sling and has started to wave his arm about.

He waves it about in a hostile manner if anything or anybody touches the top of his sore foot.

Mum gives him an **exasperated** look, and bosses him.

"If you stopped putting your foot in people's way," she tells him in a cross-patch voice, "it wouldn't get bumped."

UNFORTUNATELY My mother is not a kindly role model in the home nursing department. (For further information on this subject, Google "Florence Nightingale".)

FLORENCE NOTINGALE

The Brat's enjoying having Dad as a goofy television-watching companion.

He's happy for her to use the remotes, and she gets to watch all the programmes or videos that she likes.

And I'm sorry to say Dad was spotted twirling around a ballerina Barbie doll while they were watching a Barbie video.

Fletch and I think this is a bit of a worry.

After tea, when darkness is starting to creep down, Fletch and I sneak one of Dad's fishing rods. We stick it through the hole in the tea chest, so it makes contact with the inner workings of the ESM.

"That'll do the trick," Fletch says in a confident voice. "All that needs to happen now is for the thunderstorm to arrive."

OFF TO BED

fletch, Snoops and I go to bed at 8.37 pm. Snoops snuggles up with his head on my pillow.

I say to him, "Get off there."

But he just laughs. "*Har! Wuffy! Har! Har!*" and refuses to move.

Rather than be accused of animal cruelty, I share my pillow with Snoops.

Fletch and I read *The Wierdo Weekly Wag* magazines while we wait for the thunderstorm to arrive.

I'm reading a fascinating article about a man called Roscoe Barrington Mangrove Simpleton, who reckons he's discovered a method of transporting his mind from one country to another while his sleeping body stays in bed — he says it's called **Travel Dreaming** and is a very economical way of seeing the world.

And you don't need official stuff like passports and travel visas.

I'm about to try mind-transporting myself from Inner Mongolia to Iceland when Mum tells us to turn out the light.

"You two get some sleep." she says. "I've got some jobs lined up for you boys tomorrow — so refresh yourselves please."

Fletch makes a protest groaning noise, which makes Mum laugh . . .

"Oh no," I say in my grumpiest voice. "That's **not** fair. I'm supposed to be on **holiday**. Can't you save the slavery bit for later?"

"I'm supposed to be on holiday too," says Mum while waving a school-teachery finger at me. "Unfortunately you're the **only able-bodied male** in the house, so you will have to postpone any further holiday plans until your father's **back on deck**."

Grumble, moan and groan . . . there are times in my life when I wish my mother was not so **dependent** on me.

ACTION STATIONS

The time is 10.48 pm
The situation: Fletch and Snoops are snoring.

 I have to stay awake.

 It's my duty to turn on the ESM.

THOUGHT I wish I was asleep.

Then, without realising it I must have momentarily closed my eyes and fallen into a deep dream-land trance. I'm dreaming that I'm following in *Weirdo* Roscoe Simpleton's footsteps and am about to fly over China in the hope of spotting a Panda bear in its natural habitat, when I hear a whimpering noise.

At first I think it might be a Panda bear, but then I feel a wet-sloppy-rough tongue licking my neck and a back-to-reality thought enters my slumbering brain.

"Jeez, Snoops," I mutter. "Stop it — I don't need a bath."

It's then I hear the distant rumbling of THUNDER.

"Yay," I say and leap out of bed and turn on the ESM.

Next up, I open the window enough to stick my head out, and I'm chuffed to hear the sound of the vacuum cleaner in action.

When I climb back into bed, I find that Snoops (who is scared of thunder) has buried himself under the duvet cover. He's shivering and making wee *wuffing* noises.

I give him a pat and assure him, "I'll look after you, little fellah."

It's while I'm patting Snoops that a huge horrible mean clap of thunder comes ripping through the sky and echoes about like the sound of a big bass drum . . .

GRUMBLE RUMBLE roar BANG
CRASH and BANG
some more.

At the same time a huge flash of lightning strikes close by — it's so bright it lights up my bedroom, and sends Snoops scurrying even further under the covers.

It also wakes up Fletch.

"Creepers," he says, "that was scary."

"Yeah," I say. "The storm must be overhead. I reckon that one must've got our lightning attractor."

When I say those words another big RUMBLE rips across the sky.

Then a thought hits home . . .

"We better hope the power doesn't go off," I say to Fletch. "If it does, that means the ESM will stop working."

I hear Fletch say a minor bleep word (for your information a bleep = an unacceptable language word). Then he confesses, "I never thought of that, and just about every time we get a decent thunderstorm the power goes off."

"We might have to get one of those battery vacs," I suggest.

"Yeah," says Fletch, "but I don't know if it would have enough suction and storage capacity, and also we'd have to buy one." He sighs. "And we haven't got sufficient capital for such major expenditure."

He gets out of bed and walks over to the window.

Next minute another bolt of lightning strikes . . .

"Radical," says Fletch. "That was a real beauty. There must be enough electricity out there to fill up the ESM in no time at all." He opens the window to see if the ESM is still functioning.

For a moment there's silence, and then I hear his voice.

"Hey," he says in an urgent whispering tone, "there's somebody out there."

"Out where?" I ask.

"Outside. I can see a dark shape moving about in the driveway."

"Are you sure?" I question.

"Yeah," he says. "*Shhh*, be quiet and come and have a look!"

Like James Bond in action I slide silently out of bed, and join Fletch at the window . . .

■104

Outside the sky **BOOOMMMMS** with thunder . . . the lightning zip-zaps down to earth and lights up the backyard, and there moving ever so slowly towards the decking (just like Fletch said) is a tall, dark menacing figure.

"Bleepers," I say in a quiet voice. "It must be a burglar!"

"What'll we do?" Fletch whispers. "He looks like a Darth Vader type to me."

"Yeah," I say. "He's tall."

Fletch grabs hold of my arm . . .

"We'll have to do something — we can't send your dad out there with his loss of memory, dud foot and wrecked arm."

"You're right," I say in a determined voice. "We will have to deal with this burglar. But first of all, we should ring the police so we have some support troops."

"Right," says Fletch in a whispering voice, "that's exactly what I was thinking."

"Follow me," I tell him. "We'll use the phone in the dining room. But first you better shut the window, otherwise he might climb in."

Fletch is just about to slide the window shut when a creepy noise drifts in from outside: oⁿozzziiieₑe, oⁿozzziiieₑe, ⁿⁿozzziiieₑe...

I realise what it is.

It's the sound of the forest sprites, but this time instead of laughing they're calling my name.

The hairs stand up on my legs.

My heart starts to beat faster, as the words drift in from the night:

Be verrrrrrrry careful

"Helpers," says Fletch. "Did you hear that?"

"Yes," I say in an urgent tone of voice. "Quick, let's get to the phone, the **sprites are trying to warn us**. I think something **dreadful** must be going to happen — I reckon there's no time to waste."

Snoops, being a **cowardly-custard** at heart, doesn't want to stay alone.

He jumps out of bed, leans his trembling body against my right leg and pitty-paws along with us until we reach the dining room.

"Don't turn any lights on," I whisper to Fletch. "It'll just let the burglar know we're hot on his tail."

"But without light, I can't read the police station phone number in the book," Fletch states in a **perturbed** voice. "So you'll have to call the emergency number."

"Is this a life and death situation?" I question.

"It will be if that burglar gets inside the house. After all we don't know what his intentions are."

"You're right," I say. "For all we know he could be a mass murderer."

"Yeah," says Fletch. "Or worse!"

"What could be worse than a mass murderer?"

"I dunno," Fletch says. "But there must be something, and for all we know . . . HE might be it!"

"Okay," I say, "I'll do it!"

I'm about to press the emergency number button for the first time, when I hear a loud noise from just outside the back door.

BANG clunk CLATTER crash BANG.

My body freezes with fear . . .

Fletch grabs hold of my arm.

"I think he's coming up the steps," he whispers in an urgent tone.

"What should we do?" I whisper back.

Snoops gives a low growl . . .

GGGGRRR RROOOOOWW WWWLLL!

My insides start fluttering about.

"If the burglar manages to get inside, then when I give the word, we'll charge him," Fletch whispers. "Our only chance is to take him unawares."

"Good thinking," I say. "I'm with you."

flutter flicker flutter!
My heart starts to pound . . .

THUMP TICK **THUMP!**

The noise is getting closer.
I hear the door handle turn . . .

CLONK CLUMP CLONK.

 Mum must've forgotten to lock
the door.

The back door starts to open . . .
A dark shadow is standing in our
doorway, and is about to step forward when
Fletch yells, "CHARGE!"

And before I have time to think, Fletch and
I are running towards the back door at four-

hundred-and-fifty million kilometres an hour with **Wonder Dog Snoops** hot on our tail. The three of us hit the burglar with a mighty force. **BANG THUMP CRASH**

The burglar yells, "YahhhhhhhhHHHHHHH!" as he topples down the steps, and lies still on the wet concrete.

He moans, "oHHHHAHHHHoHHHH"

The kitchen light flicks on and we look around to find **Mum** standing there wearing her pink pyjamas!

"**What's going on?**" she yells in a distressed voice. "**What have you done to your father?**"

Case for the defence of

Oswald Devon Kingsford, his best friend Fletch John Jessup and Snoops, who for legal reasons shall be known by his pedigree name of Highland Bonnie Prince Charles XVII of Winchester on Brown Rye:

 We did **not** know Dad had gone outside.

 We did **not** realise that the storm had woken him up, and that he had looked out his bedroom window onto the decking, and saw a huge flash of lightning strike his fishing rod.

 How were we to know this would concern him, and he would feel the need to go outside and investigate?

 We thought he was sound asleep in his bed.

We were doing our duty by trying to protect our property.

Most of Dad's injuries were minor, and it should be noted he did not need professional medical attention.

 And seeing that the fall down the steps cured his memory loss, we should actually be rewarded instead of punished.

 And he should have turned on the outside light and then we would have been able to identify him!

With all possible scenarios taken into consideration the defendants ask the jury to return a finding of No case to answer.

ROCKY TIMES TWO

The time is 9.24 am on whatever day it is.

I have to say, I am too tired and disillusioned with life to care.

 Dad is back to his old, mean, tyrannical self.

He insists we dismantle the ESM.
And then gives us a stern lecture.
"You two should know better than to muck about with electrical stuff." He holds

up a sizzled looking fishing rod that sags in the middle. "And it's not a good idea to use my best fishing rod to attract lightning."

Next he points a serious finger at us. "In future I expect you to show more responsibility and to check with your mother or me before undertaking experiments such as this . . . DO YOU HEAR ME?"

"Yes, Dad," I say.

"Yes, Mister Kingsford," says Fletch.

And **unfortunately** having had his memory refreshed, he also recalls that he didn't give us permission to use his workshop.

"You do realise I **have** to punish you boys?" he says in a stern tone of voice.

At times like this it's best to be submissive.

I bow my head and say, "Yes, Dad."

Fletch follows my lead and says, "Yes, Mister Kingsford."

Then Dad says in a bossy tone, "Righto, you two follow me."

He limps out the back door.

We go next door to Missus Hobbs' house.

He knocks on the door, and Missus Hobbs answers straight away.

She's wearing a long white dress with yellow and orange daisies, and Cougar Cat is purring around her legs.

"And what can I do for you gentlemen?"

she questions.

"May Ozzie please borrow your wheelbarrow?" Dad asks. "His mother's changed her mind about where she wants her rock garden, so the boys have volunteered to move the rocks from around the back to the front of the section."

"Of course he can borrow it," says Missus Hobbs. "It's out in the wood shed, just help yourself."

"But, but, but," I say in an earnest tone of voice, "we suggested the rock garden should be around the front, but Mum said no. I don't reckon it's fair that we have to move those rocks all over again."

Dad points a serious finger at Fletch and me. "You made a decision to pull the wool over your mother's eyes, and that's called taking advantage." Then he looks at Fletch.

"As an honorary member of this family you have to share the good **and the bad sides** of Kingsford family life." He turns towards Missus Hobbs and says, "Does that sound like logical thinking?"

"Yes," says Missus Hobbs while nodding her head. "Young people need to learn to be responsible for their actions."

"Exactly," Dad says while pulling his tummy in and putting his shoulders back. "I'm bigger, bossier, older and wiser than you." He points towards the wood shed where the wheelbarrow stands ready for action.

"SO HOP TO IT!"

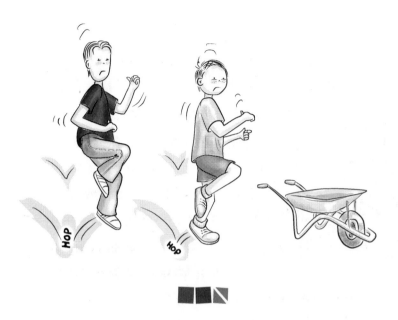

It's now 11.53 am.

Mum says we can knock off for lunch at twelve then finish the rest this afternoon.

"This is tough going. I'm sure there are **more** rocks than we had before," says Fletch while rubbing his aching arms.

"I reckon you're right," I say. "It's almost like someone keeps adding more rocks."

When I say those words I hear a distant
"Har! Har! Har!"

Fletch and I look at each other . . .

"Sprites couldn't lift rocks this big, could they?" he questions.

"Not unless there was a team of them," I say.

"But we'd see the rocks move," Fletch says while looking about.

"Yeah," I say in a positive tone of voice. "They couldn't move rocks about without somebody seeing."

It's now 12.05 pm.

We stop work and have cheese and pineapple toasted sandwiches for lunch.

Mum tells us Dad and **The Brat** have gone out on a **mission**.

"What sort of mission?" I question.

"I honestly don't know," Mum confesses. "Your father is being most mysterious."

"Do you reckon he's thinking straight?" I ask.

Mum nods her head. "Yes, he's mostly back to his normal self. You boys certainly sorted his memory loss out."

"We really did think he was a burglar," Fletch says.

"Yeah," I say. "Why didn't he turn the lights on?"

Mum frowns and says, "I don't know." Then she sighs, reaches out and ruffles my hair. "My giddiness, it's been a mucked-up few days, but things will come right."

It's now 2.14 pm.

The sun is now piping hot . . .

Mum comes out to see how we're getting on.

"You've still got an awful lot of rocks to move," she says in a surprised tone of voice. "It seems to be taking you a long time."

"I know," I say. "I'm sure these rocks have

multiplied since we carted them over."

"Oh well," she says. "A bit of hard work never hurt anyone, just keep your sun hats on and remember to drink plenty of water."

It's now 2.45 pm.

"I'm going to count the rocks we have left," says Fletch in a determined tone of voice. "Then we'll take a break and come back and count them again."

"That's good thinking," I say.

We count eighteen rocks left in the heap.

"That's my lucky number," I tell Fletch. "So I guess that means we're getting somewhere."

We go around the other side of the house and sit on the decking.

We find Snoops sprawled out asleep in the sun.

He yawns and gives us a look that plainly says: Leave me alone, I'm sleeping.

(For further information on the subject, Google "let sleeping dogs lie".)

It's now 3.05 pm.

"I count **twenty-nine** rocks," says Fletch.

"Me too," I say in agreement. "Even though it seems incredible, amazing and totally out of this world, it's got to be those **pesky sprites.**"

When I say those very words, a mean wind comes up and blows Fletch's hat off his head, a shiver runs down my body and the air fills with laughter,

"Har! Har! Har! Har! Har! Har!

Har! Har!"

"Radical," says Fletch. "It sounds like an army of them out there."

"Right," I say. "It's time to put a halt to this frivolity."

I stand on top of the pile of rocks and wave a fist in the air.

"You sprites listen to me," I yell. "This is not funny. We are worn out and have had enough of your pesky games. Do you hear me?" I wave my hand about some more, and yell, "I want you to GO AWAY!"

It's then I notice Fletch is pointing a finger.

I look in the direction his finger is pointing . . .

Mum's standing looking at me with a puzzled look on her face.

She walks over slowly and says, "Are you feeling okay, Ozzie?"

Never being one to miss out on an

opportunity I rub my brow and say, "OH! OH! OH!" Then I groan as I sink to my knees. "It must be the heat getting to me."

Fletch puts a concerned look on his face and says to my mother, "Ozzie's gone a bit loopy. I reckon he must be suffering from juvenile overwork syndrome."

"Really?" says Mum looking concerned. She leans forward and ruffles my hair in a sympathetic manner. "Well, I think you boys better come inside out of the heat . . . I'll make you a nice cold drink — moving the rest of the rocks can wait for another day."

DAD SPRINGS A SURPRISE

it is 4.33 pm when Dad arrives home with **The Brat**.

Fortunately, Mum tells him about me suffering from a near-lethal dose of heat stroke. Dad tells us not to worry — he'll give us a hand to move the rest of the rocks another time.

Then he says to **The Brat**, "Come on, sweetie, give your mum her present."

Dad is the only person in the whole world who calls **The Brat** a *sweetie*.

I reckon it must be because he's short-sighted. Har! Har!

"What present?" Mum asks.

The Brat hands over a white envelope and says in her squeaky voice, "This is from Dad for his best wife and family."

Mum laughs. "Well, well," she says, "I wonder what's in here."

She opens the envelope and pulls out a brochure for *Shark Tooth Bay Wilderness Camping Ground.*

I see a confused look flash across her face.

"I tried to re-book our luxury holiday,"

Dad says, "but there's nothing going. So it's back to Mother Nature at Shark Tooth Bay — plenty of fresh sea air, good fishing and we can make our own luxuries. There's a caravan and tent booked for six days from tomorrow so we'd better get packing."

He points a serious finger at Snoops, "Snoops you can come too, but you have to be kept under control at all times — do you hear me?"

Snoops gives Dad a solemn dog-eye look, and nods his head.

Mum doesn't say one word. I see a look of **shock** mixed with **horror** flash across her face, and I figure this news has left her speechless.

Dad looks at Fletch and says, "By the way, I stopped by your folks' place and they said you can come too!"

"YAY!" I yell. "Choice, man!"

Fletch turns pink with pleasure.

The Brat complains, "It's not fair — I wanted Primrose to come too, but Dad said NO!"

Snoops, who can no longer contain his joy,

gives a *"Yip, yap, wuff, snuffle, huff and wuff."*

Which means: "Hurrah! I'm going on holiday."

ROCKY TIMES THREE

7he time is 7.32am.
Fletch, Snoops and I have just woken up.

I pull the curtains and the sun shines through the window.

Next minute there's the sound of heavy footsteps down the hallway and then Dad puts his head around our bedroom door and yells,

"Right, you boys rise and **shine.** No mucking around, you

have **one** hour to get breakfasted, dressed and in the car."

Then Mum, who is looking a bit worn out after spending half the night sorting out essential gear for our holiday, pops her head in our door and says, "I've just been out the back and I'm **really impressed**, but remember Dad did say he would help you."

"Help us with what?" I question.

"Moving the rest of the rocks," she gives us a beaming smile and adds. "But it's nice to know you boys are developing a responsible attitude."

When she's gone Fletch and I look at each other with eyes wide open.

"Come on," I say in an urgent tone of

voice, "we'd better check this out."

We race down the hallway at one-and-a-quarter million kilometres per hour.

Out the back door, around the corner and down the back to where the rocks were stacked and there's **NOT ONE** rock to be seen.

"Jeez-helpers," says Fletch, "I don't **believe** this!"

"Nor me," I say.

"Do you reckon it was the sprites?"

"It must have been."

A soft, warm wind blows.

The branches on the trees whisper in the wind.

Fletch gives me the thumbs up and sits down on the ground.

"They're loitering around here somewhere," he says. "See if you can get them to talk to you."

"Okay," I say, and I lower my voice and speak into the wind. "Hello you sprites . . . thank you for moving the rest of the rocks."

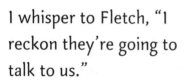

I stand still and listen.
My eyes don't blink.
My heart beats
slowly . . . *pit . . . pat*
. . . *pit . . . pat.*

I whisper to Fletch, "I reckon they're going to talk to us."

"Do you?" he whispers back.

"Yes," I say in a hushed voice. "I can feel voice vibrations in the air."

And I was right.

I *did* feel vibrations in the air.

But instead of sprite-talk, the air around us is suddenly filled with tyrannical Attila-the-Hun-foghorn-voice-vibrations.

"IS THIS ROCK BUSINESS YOUR IDEA OF A JOKE?"

Dad's voice is *reallyreallyreally* angry.

"What joke?" I exclaim.

"Why on earth would you want to stack a whole heap of rocks in **the middle of the driveway?** How am I supposed to get the car out?"

A stunned look flashes across Fletch's face . . .

"But, but, but, **we didn't**," I protest.

"So **WHO DID?**" Dad yells, his voice now rising to **sonic-boom** level.

There's a silence.

I'm about to put on my **Ultimate Defence**

Attorney voice, but reality hits and my heart flops over inside my body.

 Nobody will believe us.

Question: How can you explain the unexplainable?

 I know what my dad is going to say next.

Fletch gives me a sympathetic look . . .

Dad points a serious finger. "You have **one** hour to clear those rocks off the driveway, so **GET CRACKING!**"

8.23 am: We lift the first rock.

9.15 am: I've now lifted at least **one ton** of rocks. I'm tired, worn out and exhausted. Fletch mops his brow and says he's suffering from a triple dose of juvenile overwork syndrome.

Snoops, who's been watching us work, puts a mournful look on his face. I think he knows we've been **falsely accused.**

 Can dogs see sprites?

9.35 am: Mum comes out and gives us a cold drink of water and then shakes her head. "I don't know why you boys would want to do such an irresponsible thing," she says. "And just to think, I thought you'd developed a smidgeon of dependability."

9.40 am: The Brat puts her head out the window and yells, "Hurry up, you big dummy-bummies, we want to go on holiday."

"She's a real charmer, your sister," says Fletch.

"Yeah," I say. "But Mum reckons deep down inside she secretly loves us!"

Fletch laughs, and we roll our eyes at each other . . .

9.55 am: Dad yells out, "You've got TEN minutes to finish up, or we'll go without you."

10.05 am: There are two left to move.

Fletch picks up the first rock.

I pick up the second rock.

We walk together and place the rocks on the pile.

"Helpers," I say. "I hope those sprites don't come on holiday with us."

"Yeah," says Fletch. "I think my body is broken."

"You're a good mate," I tell him.

Fletch's face lights up . . . he grins and gives me a thump on the shoulder.

Snoops scampers towards us, his eyes are bright and shiny.

He dances in circles and tells us, "*Wuff, ruff, woof, ruff, wuff.*"

This in doggy language means: Hurry up, or

we'll get left behind.

It's then I hear the car motor start, and next second see the station wagon backing down the driveway . . . Dad stops and yells out, "Are you three coming?"

"Wuff, ruff," says Snoops and fast-paws it towards the car.

I put my left hand on Fletch's shoulder . . .

"I reckon we should start this day all over again," I say. "It can only get better." Fletch rolls his eyes . . .

We both stand to attention and give our Boy Scout salutes.

Then we grin at each other and shout out in unison, "Shark Tooth Bay, here we come! WHOOPPPPEEEE!"

COMING SOON

A Shark Tooth Bay Holiday in the Life of Ozzie Kingsford.

Ozzie's golf-nutter dad secretly organises a holiday at a rough-and-rugged faraway wilderness known as Shark Tooth Bay.

Fletch and Ozzie meet a leathery old man who warns them about the monster inhabitants of caves that dot the cliff face.

In search of monsters and using their Ultimate Boy Scout skills, Ozzie and Fletch sneak out in the darkness of the night, and

this sneaky sneakiness leads to a series of very
UNFORTUNATE events.

LOOK OUT FOR MORE TITLES IN THE OZZIE KINGSFORD SERIES!

A Birthday in the Life of Ozzie Knigsford

Five (and a bit) Days in the Life of Ozzie Kingsford

A Shark Tooth Bay Holiday in the Life of Ozzie Kingsford

ABOUT THE AUTHOR

Val Bird spent her childhood years in Hastings, before settling in the seaside town of Whakatane — where she lives in a nice quiet house with husband Ros, two big hairy dogs (Fudge and Wally) and a crazy, bed-hogging, tabby cat called Candy-kit.

One day her daughter Rebecca asked Val to write a children's book that she could illustrate. At the time Val thought, "Oh my giddiness, can I do that?" And yes, it turned out (after a few false starts) that indeed she could, and that's how Ozzie Kingsford and his entertaining family came to life.

Val would like to thank Random House for recognising Ozzie's potential and hopes in the future you (the reader) will enjoy further adventures with the Kingsford family.

ABOUT THE ILLUSTRATOR

Born in Hastings, raised in Whakatane, Rebecca Cundy is married to Troy and lives in a very happy house. When not working or mothering daughters Hannah and Brooklyn, she spends time patting the cat, walking on the beach, and having fun.

As a child Rebecca spent hours and hours drawing cartoon characters, which started her off on a pathway to graphic design. Now in her thirties, she is delighted to call herself a Children's Book Illustrator. Yes, dreams

combined with hard work do come true.
Rebecca hopes you will enjoy the Kingsford
family characters as much as she enjoyed
creating them.